D1642601

Muckeen and the UFO

• Words and pictures •
by Fergus Lyons

THE O'BRIEN PRESS
DUBLIN

First published 2004 by The O'Brien Press Ltd,
12 Terenure Road East, Rathgar, Dublin 6, Ireland.
Tel: +353 1 4923333; Fax: +353 1 4922777
E-mail: books@obrien.ie
Website: www.obrien.ie
Reprinted 2005, 2006.

ISBN-10: 0-86278-832-3
ISBN-13: 978-0-86278-832-2

British Library Cataloguing-in-Publication Data
Lyons, Fergus
Muckeen and the UFO
(Panda series ; 28)
1.Children's stories
I.Title
823.9'14[J]

The O'Brien Press receives assistance from

3 4 5 6 7 8 9 10
06 07 08 09 10

Typesetting, layout, editing, design: The O'Brien Press Ltd
Printing: Cox & Wyman Ltd

Can YOU spot the panda
hidden in the story?

Muckeen was in the **Big Field**
behind the farmhouse.
It was a lovely day
for dancing and skipping.

Muckeen was excited
because it was nearly dinner time.
Time for Mrs Farmer to bring him
lovely **sloppy stuff**
in a bucket.

Sloppy stuff was Muckeen's
favourite dinner.
Just thinking about it
made him happy.
So he was dancing
around in circles
with his eyes closed.

The chickens were watching
Muckeen dancing.
They didn't notice
the big silver **UFO**
hovering in the sky above them.
It had come from
outer space.

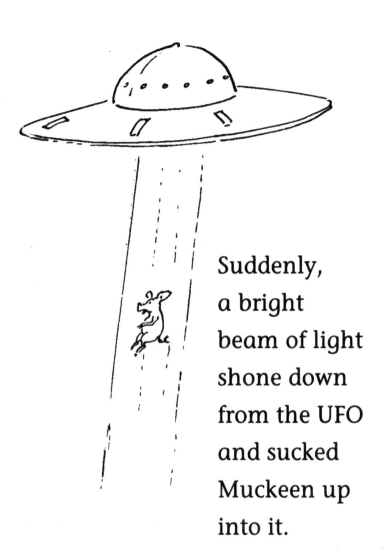

Suddenly,
a bright
beam of light
shone down
from the UFO
and sucked
Muckeen up
into it.

10

Then, with Muckeen on board,
the UFO flew away.

The chickens
could not understand
what had happened.
They stood looking at
the burnt patch of grass
where Muckeen had just been.
Then Mrs Farmer arrived
with Muckeen's dinner.

When Mrs Farmer saw that
Muckeen wasn't there,
she put down the bucket
and began to cry.
Muckeen always came running
for his dinner.
And now where was he?
He was **gone**.

Something terrible
must have happened
to her little Muckeen!

Mrs Farmer saw
the burnt patch of grass.
She thought that maybe
somebody had come along
and **cooked** and **eaten** him!

Meanwhile, on the UFO,
Muckeen was also wondering
what had happened.

One minute he was
dancing and skipping
in the Big Field,
and now where was he?
At first he thought that
too much twirling in circles
had made him dizzy
and that he had fainted.

19

He looked around
and saw that he was no longer
in the Big Field.
Instead, he was on board
a **spaceship**.
There were lots of round
windows in the spaceship,
and Muckeen looked out of one.
What he saw gave him
a **terrible fright**.

Down below was the farmhouse,
and the Big Field,
and the chickens,
and Mrs Farmer
with his dinner bucket
full of **sloppy stuff**.
They were all so far away,
and getting further
by the second.

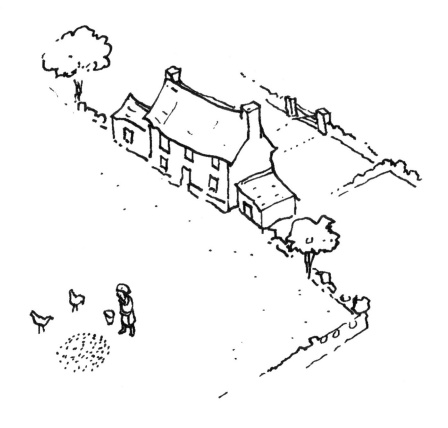

Muckeen kept looking,
with his nose pressed
to the window.

Soon all he could see
were **stars** whizzing by.

Then he heard some footsteps
behind him.

Muckeen turned around
and saw a sight
he had never seen before.
It was a group of **aliens**
and he was on
their spaceship.

They said nothing.
They stood staring at him.

Then one of them
stepped forward.
Muckeen began to
squeal with fright.

He squealed as loudly as he could.

It was such a horrible noise!

All the aliens ran away
with their hands over their ears.

Muckeen felt a whole lot better.
If squealing at the aliens
upset them so much,
they might even take him back
to the Big Field
just to get rid of him.

Then some of the aliens returned.
One of them started
to make funny sounds.
He was **talking** to Muckeen.

But it was no use.
To Muckeen,
alien speech sounded
just like frogs
hopping in and out
of cold porridge.
Plop! Plop! Plop!
Muckeen could not understand
a single word.

One of the aliens
was holding a silver bowl
with wires sticking out of it.
The alien offered the bowl
to Muckeen,
and he quickly took it.
He thought there might be
some **sloppy stuff** in it
for him to eat.
But there wasn't.

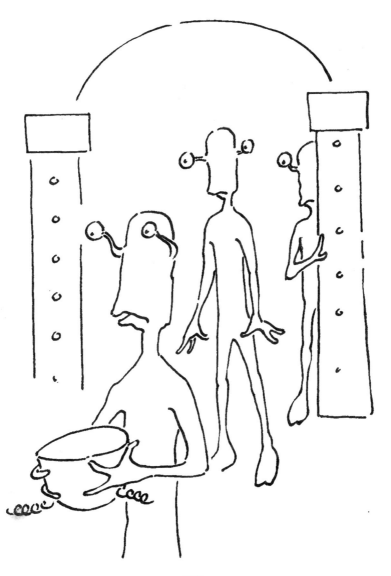

The alien wanted Muckeen
to place the silver thing
on his head,
like a hat.

Muckeen loved hats.
He had always wanted
to have one for himself.
So he put it on.
But the thing **was not** a hat.

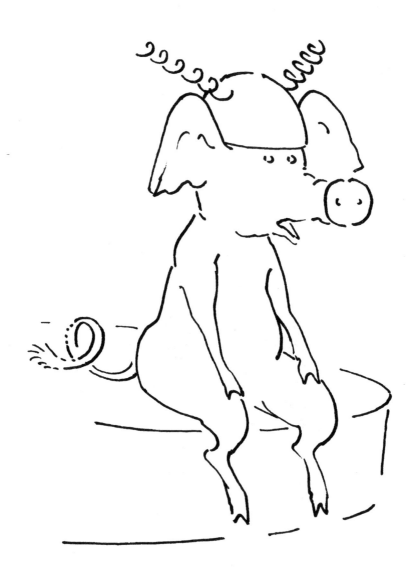

It was a
special alien machine.
If you put it on your head,
you could understand
alien language.
Now Muckeen could
talk to the aliens.

'Do not be afraid,'
said the alien.
'We will not harm you.
We want you to help us
if you can.
Please can you help us?
Please?'

Then they all joined in.
'We are not happy,'
they explained.
'Nobody is happy
where we come from.'

And that was their problem.
They told Muckeen that
they were **super-intelligent**
and had nearly everything
that they could ever need,
but still they were not happy.

'We **worry** about everything,
all the time,' they said.
'We never stop **worrying**.
We want to learn to be happy,
just like you.'

Muckeen was delighted
that they wanted him
to teach them.
This was a very important job.
First, he showed the aliens
how to skip around.

45

The aliens tried to skip.
They were very stiff
and serious at the beginning,
but they kept trying.
With Muckeen's help,
they were all soon skipping
up and down,
all around the spaceship.

Next, Muckeen showed them
how to dance.
The aliens were amazed!
There was no dancing
where they came from.
They all wanted to try.
So Muckeen taught them,
one by one.

They were having so much fun!
Then one of the aliens
had a great idea.
Using a special machine
that could make
all sorts of things,
he made
a whole lot of funny hats.
There was a hat for everyone
on board the spaceship,
including Muckeen.

Muckeen loved his new hat.
It was exactly the kind
he had always wanted.

So, wearing their funny hats
and dancing and skipping around,
they all had a **great party**.

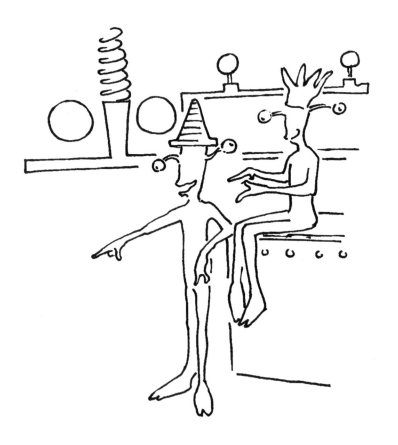

54

When the party was over
the aliens said they would
teach everyone on their planet
how to have fun too.
They asked Muckeen
if he would like to
come along with them.
He was tempted to go
but decided not to.
He thought there might be
no **sloppy stuff** there.

So before they set out
on the long journey
to their home
on the far side of the stars,
the aliens flew Muckeen
back to the farm.
They said goodbye
and carefully lowered him
to the ground
on a beam of light.

Then they were gone ...

... to the stars and beyond.

When Mrs Farmer looked out
the kitchen window,
who did she see but Muckeen!

He was sitting
in the middle of the Big Field
looking a bit dizzy.

With a shout of surprise
and delight
she called to Mr Farmer,
'Muckeen is back!'
Then she ran outside
carrying the bucket
full of **sloppy stuff**.

Mr and Mrs Farmer
were very happy
that Muckeen had returned.
But they never did find out
where he had been ...

... or where he had got the hat.